Death Expectancy

"And what would you say my life expectancy would be, Mama Naomi?"

"You ain't got no life expectancy, Mon. You got a death expectancy."

A tale of voodoo and psychic experiences

Contents

About the author

CD Moulton has traveled extensively over much of the world both in the music business, where he was a rock guitarist, songwriter and arranger and in an import/export business. He has been everything from a bar owner to auto salvage (junkyard) manager, longshoreman to high steel worker, orchid grower to landscaper, tropical fish farmer to commercial fisherman. He started writing books in 1983 and has published more than 350 books as of January 1, 2023. His most popular books to date are about research with orchids, though much of his science fiction and fantasy work has proven popular. He wrote the CD Grimes, PI series, and the Det. Nick Storie series, Clint Faraday series, and many other works.

He now resides in Gualaca, Chiriqui, Panamá, where he writes books, plays music with friends, does research with orchids and medicinal plants. He has lately become involved in fighting for the rights of the indigenous people, who are among his closest friends, and in fighting the extreme corruption in the courts and police in Panamá.

He offers the free e-book, *Fading Paradise*, that explains what he has been through because of the corruption.

CD is the discoverer of the Chadam Protocol for curing cancer.

Facebook page Ambrosia peruviana for cancer.

<u>*Caribbean Cruise*</u>

Wilson Farmer leaned over the rail on the upper deck to look down at the wharf. Francine and her mother, Wila, were just spots, more than a figure. She had her little folding binoculars focused on him and waved. He waved back.

This liner was big. Two Olympic-sized swimming pools on this deck.

He wasn't really enthused about going on this cruise. Francine was like looking at people from a long city block away. He was actually that far above her.

It wasn't far enough. He won this cruise at a raffle at the children's fair. Two weeks cruising the Caribbean, all expenses paid – for one. Donated by Fairy Princess Lines to raise money for medical research into children's diseases. The gimmick was that they had it all paid for one, but most would want someone along, so the line made out on what the other(s) paid.

He had the money to bring Francine and her mother along, but they didn't know that. He had managed to keep a secret account with more than sixty thousand in it from anyone's knowledge. The only reason he was taking this cruise was to get away from Francine. From Wila, actually.

Francine was a pretty girl with a sweet personality. They would probably get along very well as very close friends for life, but Mama inserted herself into it. She was determined that Will was going to marry Francine. She had more and more gotten control of both their lives. What had started as a good thing had turned into Hell. He didn't have a minute's freedom. He suspected Francine wasn't as keen on the deal as she acted, but she was as much as terrified of her mother and wanted out.

When he met Wila, he got the first flash in a long time. He had a couple of incidents in his past when he met a person. A sign of some sort flashed across their face. It didn't last more than a tenth of a second, but he found it was generally accurate. Wila, a cobra poised to strike. He got more and more of the flashes, lately.

One time, when Mama was in New Orleans for the night, Francine had said she was out of range. They had to find some way to get her mother out of their relationship, that Mama was destroying their chances to be happy. He didn't want to live his life with her and she didn't want to live hers with him.

Then it was back. The feeling they were being watched. For a few seconds it had been gone.

He hadn't answered. He had slightly nodded.

Mama Wila LeDuc had an uncanny way to know whatever they said. Francine said she was a witch who had fallen in love and lost her power. She was a result of that love affair. It had grown stale and her father had died. There had never been an explanation for his death. He had fallen from the dock and drowned before anyone could get to him – even though he was an excellent swimmer. He was walking along the dock and had simply fallen. There wasn't a mark on his body. He didn't have a heart attack or an embolism or anything else. He had fallen in the water and died. The medical examiner said he had to put something on the death certificate, and he was in the water. There wasn't really evidence that he died from drowning.

The doctor had questioned Francine about her father. She was just nine years old. The doctor had practiced medicine for years in New Orleans. He told Francine to be very careful. What he had seen in the past fit too well. Her father had died from a voodoo curse. The doctor had spent his first fifteen years in New Orleans debunking voodoo murders, but he had to admit that about ten percent of them left no explanation of the cause of death. This was such a case.

Francine knew her mother and father had fallen out of love. They argued a lot.

When her mother had fallen out of love, half her power returned. She would never be among the very powerful again, but she had some. She had tried to pass it to Francine, but Francine didn't have the natural power, so would never be able to build it.

She suggested she wished she had a natural power. She wouldn't have to put up with what her life had become. Mama wouldn't be running her life.

The ramp was withdrawn. Francine waved again. Will had a sudden vertigo attack. He clung to the rail and fought it.

He had known the first time he had one of the attacks that they came from outside. It was when he had just met Francine and decided he would like to know her better.

He remembered that. He had met Francine at a little fair where he was working. He was with his father, who had been with the carnival for years. His mother had been the fortune teller until the train wreck, where she was killed. His father guessed your weight and age or you won a cigar or something. He was good at that. His father showed him things that happened as you aged. It was always within a year. The cellulite cells, the waist moving up, the little signs no one noticed. The weight was a matter of figuring volume. That was easy enough.

Then you had to know when a woman, in particular, but sometimes a man, were lying about their age. If she dyed her hair and wore a girdle and a thousand other clues, you took as many years from the age as you felt she was trying to get away with. "Hmmm. You're a little older than you tell people (she will look nervous). You're twenty eight!" She's, according to the signs, thirty five. She will gush and say he was right. She told people she was twenty six, but she was actually twenty eight. Almost twenty nine.

You also had a feeling that, in his father, was always on the money. He knew, automatically, how old a person was. Within a few days. He said it was a talent he was born with. His mother had an ability to know how a person's love life would be. She just knew. She had to do the fortune teller bit to make a living, but had a reputation for being a hundred percent.

"Honey, what you do when you see this or that one is doomed, is tell them they have a dark cloud they must avoid. If they make the right choices and let their mind rule over their hearts when there is a question, they will have a bright future. If they don't do that, that dark cloud is there. Beware!

"They will, of course, make all the wrong decisions and be miserable, but you were right! You tried to warn them!"

He had a little ability. He could sense when a person was lying in some scam to try to take advantage of him, for money or whatever. He had a natural resistance.

When he first met Wila, he got that feeling. It was strong. Here was a woman who was all smiles and pleasantries who had an agenda. She was also a little scared. He figured because she wanted to run Francine's life and to choose her friends and it wasn't going to work with him.

He wished it had.

This cruise, he would be out of her area of influence, as he called it. He would be careful, because Francine couldn't escape. The last thing he wanted was for her to be hurt.

The ship moved from the wharf. People were walking off the end into the city. Everyone moved away from the rail. He waited until the vertigo passed and went toward his cabin. A very pretty, sexy girl gave him an obvious look. He saw a dollar sign across her face for a split second. She was a prostitute.

He smiled at her and went on.

It was almost an hour before the feeling of being watched faded. Just before it was completely gone he saw a huge ball of fire coming directly toward him. He pictured a ball of water going toward the ball of fire. They collided. He staggered. A spear of the fire came toward him. He jerked back at the last second and it went into the wall.

Nothing like that had ever happened to him before. He didn't know where the water ball came from in his mind, but knew it was a natural defense. Small things had happened all his life where such things occurred. It was a talent from his parents that protected him. Someone – or something – had tried to kill him there. He was strong enough to thwart it.

People were staring at him.

"Touch of vertigo," he said. "I have to expect it at times. It's not serious, but people will think I'm drunk or something. It can be embarrassing."

A woman said her aunt had that. It was caused by a heart valve flutter. She had an operation for it.

"An operation that costs on the order of thirty thousand dollars, which I don't have a third of," he replied. They both laughed.

He went on to the restaurant for a delicious Porterhouse steak. The food served on these cruises was legendary. He then went down to the ballroom to mingle and meet people. He was attractive enough that he soon had several women giving him speculative looks. They were on a vacation and were looking for some diversion. That was what these cruises were about for many. Let loose, remember to take the pill, and have some fun.

A dark woman came to look him over. He saw a viper across her face for a split second. He had never seen that one before, but it was plain what it meant.

"Hi. I'm Georgette. You are?"

"From hunger, but my name is Bill."

She smiled. "That is not your name."

"And Georgette is not yours."

She got a very hard look for a second, then smiled. "These cruises are for anonymous fun."

"I wish you a lot of that."

"May I offer you a drink?" There was a skull and crossbones across her face for the flash. She was planning on poisoning him? Why?

"No."

She looked confused. The hard look was back. "Why not?"

He didn't know why he said it. "Because I have the power."

She looked scared. She turned and walked off.

A big black man standing close asked him if he was gay.

He saw a dollar sign across his face for the flash. "No. Why?"

"You just ran a fine piece of ass away. You could see she wanted you."

He laughed. "I love you, Honey. I love your money – which I ain't got much of."

"I wouldn't have pictured her as a pro. She's hot."

"You don't picture you as a pro, but it's what you do. As I told her, I have the power."

He laughed. "Whatever works. I have to make a living, same as anyone else."

"I hope you make a good one. Save as much as you can. You won't always be a young handsome hunk."

"Happens to all of us. I do save most of it. I don't think I'll like working for a living.

"Can I buy you a drink?"

"No one buys drinks here, but I'd like a Vodka Collins, I think. Tall and cool and lots of ice."

"You don't buy bar booze. Stolichnaya costs two bucks a shot."

"They pour Smirnoff. Who needs more?"

They chatted. Buck was a lot of fun. He met an older woman wearing a lot of expensive jewelry, winked, and said they would talk later.

A heavy black woman in a bright flowered skirt and big floppy hat with hibiscus and ribbons came to say Buck was alright. He was her nephew. She was the mystical fortune teller with mighty powers for this ship. He wasn't bullshitting when he told that French voodoo woman and Buck he had the power.

"What's your talent?" he asked. "I'm Wilson Farmer."

"What *am* you name, Mon. I'm Mama Naomi. I knows how long a person lives before he croaks."

"Good way to make a bundle. Work for an insurance company. Know how long a life expectancy is and turn down the ones who won't live long enough to make a profit from."

"If I didn't have no morals. I ain't makin' no greedy company any richer than they are. Mebbe I'd turn down the ones what live a long time 'n get the ones who'll croak next year! Break their greedy asses fine!"

He laughed.

"What you talent, Mon?"

"I see what a person really is, sometimes. I saw a snake with Georgette, and a skull and crossbones. With Buck, dollar signs. With you, a happy face."

"Georgette be dangerous. Two people die she with. It ain't no heart attack, lessen the heart were attacked by poison. She don't work none for herself. So who done decided you better for them dead?"

"I can think of one. Mama Wila. New Orleans."

"Don't know of 'er. Not much power."

"She used to have it, but fell in love. He died for no reason when she fell out of love. Has a daughter I like, but she gets in the way all the time. What could have been never will be."

She nodded. "What sign you get from that one?" she pointed to a bimbo-type blond talking with an old man. The man was wearing a Rolex and a casual shirt by Armani or something.

"You need a sign? Hundred dollar bills falling from the sky!"

She laughed. "You is right. I don't need no sign 'bout that one!"

"So! What's my life expectancy, Mama Naomi?"

"You ain't got no life expectancy, Mon. You got a death expectancy!"

"That mean anything?"

"Same thing. I can't find no life or no death expectancy from one what got the power, an' you sure as sunset got power!

"You a good man. I ain't got no scare 'cause you got power. You got fun in you. Most what got half you power don't get no fun in life."

"No fun, why bother living?"

"You is real. I like you, Mon!" She jerked back, then hissed, "Take care!"

"I felt that, too. It was pure rage. I don't know where it was from!"

She went into some kind of trance. Will wasn't sure it wasn't an act, but he felt he could trust Mama Naomi. She shook and muttered a bit, then stared him in the face.

"You die!"

She staggered and stared at him. People were muttering and staring at them.

"What I say, Mon? Ain't nothin' like that never happent before!"

"You said I'll die. We all do, sooner or later. I'm not scared by this."

"I gotta ask you. Mebbe it's from ... mebbe she save a little for one try. It done not worked. I think she ...

got pregnant? Who you got pregnant, Mon?"

"Pregnant? No one. The ones I've slept with will know how to prevent that."

"Zini. Who Zini?"

"It's what I call Francine, Wila's daughter."

"You got her pregnant?"

"No. Wila was always in the way. We didn't have any sexual relations."

"She done pregnant. Why she think it you?"

"She wouldn't. I don't get it!"

"Ah! Wila done got some power. Zini got pregnant. Wila think it you. Zini no tell her not. You got real big problem, Mon. I like you. I try to help."

What in *Hell* was going on?

Will thought about things. Francine was pregnant? Why hadn't he known about her being with anyone else?

That didn't matter. He didn't want her anymore. Wila had seen to that.

He wondered a bit about what had happened out there. Was it the use of the language when Mama Naomi said "... I think she ... got pregnant?"

That was important. She got pregnant. Not her daughter got pregnant.

He tried to think back. He remembered when he first saw Francine. It was at Jaime's birthday party. He noticed her, but she wasn't really his type.

When had he noticed her in any other way?

Two nights later. She happened to be at the Big Burger. He remembered her from the party, sort of, and said hello. She sat with him for a shake. By the end of the shake, he was a lot more interested in her.

Why? What had impressed him about her?

He couldn't remember anything more than that they were chatting about the way the French Quarter wasn't the French Quarter anymore. Something on that order. He decided to get some French fries. They ate them, and he was very interested in her.

Okay. She was lying all along, if she was pregnant.

She was using him as a buffer between someone else and her mother. She had put something in his shake when he went to get the fries. Now that he was away, he was starting to see what was going on.

Was it her, not her mother, who was causing all the crap? Why?

Because her mother wouldn't put up with her lover for ten seconds. He was there strictly to protect someone else.

Francine did have power, but she was going to lose it. Already had. She was pregnant.

So she was manipulating Wila into doing whatever she wanted done while keeping herself to the side as seemingly innocent.

"Why" was probably something he wouldn't understand. It would have to do with the power.

That rage didn't come from the place the other things were coming from.

That rage was from ... all along, there were two slightly different feelings about the watching. When he was with Francine, it was one thing. It was very slightly different when he wasn't with her, usually.

So. she was one watcher, Wila was the other.

That rage worried him. That was from Wila – and was directed at someone else.

Oh, well. He would have a little fun and come back to that later if anything more happened.

He went to the upper pool bar for a Collins and to watch the people. He saw where most of the younger women hung around. The guys and gigolos were trying to impress them.

He grinned. He went to his cabin to change into his bathing suit, slung a towel over his shoulder, and went to the pool just beside them. He kept himself in shape. He actually worked at things that kept him trim and toned. He wasn't bad to look at, and he had a few skills.

He had practiced some tightrope walking and trapeze moves. He had practiced diving from the high platform into the net. You had to know how to hit. They made a game of diving techniques out of it.

He saw he had been noticed after a few minutes, so went to the high board, bounced it a few times to get the tension rhythm of the board, then did a perfect swan to be able to gage the distance. When he climbed the ladder for the next dive he saw that most eyes were on him.

Casual. Like you're just diving for the feeling of flight.

He did a high bounce, then a toe touch, then a backward arch and hit perfectly. He swam around a minute, then went back to his chair and towel. There were several girls sitting in the near chairs all of a sudden.

He intended to enjoy this vacation. This was a great start.

Nan vanGoode was a great night.

In the morning he went back to his cabin. He dressed a bit and went to breakfast in the Dolphin Room, where he chatted with a few of the girls from the pool yesterday evening. Buck came in. They talked a bit, then Georgette came by. Will saw confusion and more than a little fear in her. She went to stand by a potted palm. It was obvious she wanted to talk to him.

What the Hell? Why not?

He strolled over to ask, "What?"

"You were dating Francine LeDuc?"

"Dating? No. I know her."

"You don't know what happened?"

"Happened? You've lost me."

"She's dead. She and her mother. It looks like they had a battle of some sort. It was with the power. Francine didn't have any power, so far as anyone knew, but she did, and was hiding it. Or something."

"Was it Francine who wanted you to poison me, or Wilma?"

She hesitated. "You have power. I don't know. I was directed. I don't believe either."

"Who else?"

"You weren't dating Francine? You weren't the father of the baby she was pregnant with?"

"Very definitely not."

"I will be safe if I get off down past the inner islands. Curacao, or close.

"There is someone very powerful who wants to be rid of you. I think it is not a woman. I think you are stronger, but don't know it. I think you are not evil. I think he is.

"You have to learn of your power and know how to use it. My ability is to see some things in the future. I can only advise. I suggest you get off this ship in Haiti or Jamaica. Go to a close small island and learn to use your power. There is a reason the person who is so afraid of you will try to find you. It is inevitable that he will. You have until that time to learn how to protect yourself from his power.

"If you are successful, I am free. If you fail, I am damned." She walked away.

Weird!

He went back to the group. They chatted awhile. Buck and Will went to the entertainment room and shot a few games of eight ball, then went to play a few hoops, then just lazed around until lunch time. Mama Naomi came to them at lunch and said there were some disturbing signs of a type she had never encountered before. She had some kind of need to advise Will about going back to New Orleans immediately, that he was needed.

Will told them about the things Georgette had said. Mama Naomi went to the computer room and contacted some people she knew in New Orleans. It was true. Wila and Francine were dead. There was a pentagram they were both drug into. They were mutilated pretty horribly.

Naomi called them into the computer room. They went into a cubicle.

She explained that she had found the urge to get Will back to New Orleans was from an evil source. It was better he did not go back yet. He must first prepare himself.

Naomi got in touch with Mama Lulu, who was a quiet witch with a lot of power. Naomi asked her how far from the scene where Wila and Francine died was she?

-Very close-

Will you go there and read it for me? It is very important to a very good person.

-Yes. One hour. I'll take the laptop and contact you while there.-

"We eat some lunch and you be back here in one hour," Naomi suggested. "This is muy scary. I not scare easy, Mon."

They said they would be there. Will and Buck had a lunch that was as good as in any gourmet restaurant, then were back. Naomi was chatting with Mama Lulu.

They done got back. Tell them.

-I am in the room. The pentagram is on the floor. It is a false diagram that has no power. I read that someone wants you to think a demon was called, but there has been no demon here. This was murder. The father ... it is not clear. Francine was ... trying to entrap ... you and another to generate power from two angles. I cannot read if it is the other person or another who did this. It is important to the one who did it that you die. He greatly fears you. Francine tricked him. She had no love, so did not lose any power. She, in fact, gained a large bit. She and Wila were going to consolidate power. They would become stronger than anyone, but were fooling only themselves. The other has more power and would not lose any. He has somehow gained even more by the deaths of Wila and Francine.-

Will got advice from Georgette, who I don't know. She got some little power. She say he go to the islands. He learn about him power. He good man. He gone need it and more added. I think so. You?

-Good advice. I sense some power, but you are far away.-

Merci. I done owe you one.

-You owe me millions, but you won't ever pay. Good luck. You are a good person.-

"He should go to Palmita," Buck said. "Aunt Bernadette?"

"I gone ask her. She got more power then anybody. We's friends and fam'ly both. She be good."

Buck grinned. "Will, my brother, you are about to spend a week or two with the most powerful voodoo queen in the islands.

"Some vacation, huh?"

"It has been interesting. I'm finding it hard to believe I'm not hallucinating or having a bad dream."

"Nan could be in a bad dream?"

"You have a point!"

"So. We be in Haiti the day after tomorrow. You go there to Palmitas with Buck. He be back here before we sails.

"Go lay a few silly girls. That what you horny men do, yah?"

"Yah!" from both Will and Buck.

Buck left Will with the happy, bubbly black woman known as Mama Bernadette – and feared by some thousands of people who knew anything about voodoo. They went to a neat little cabin under a wad of tall coconut palm trees. Mama Bernadette warned that he should always be careful under the palms. A coconut falling a hundred feet onto your head is no better than an iron ball falling a hundred feet onto your head. You're dead from either one.

She had a delicious lobster chowder prepared for dinner. They chatted about where they'd spent their pasts and things that happened in life. Bernadette had met his mother when he was four years old. She had worked the carnival for two weeks in Texas until she had the money to get back home.

When they knew each other reasonably well and could trust one another, they got around to Will's problem.

"The one who seeks your demise is hard to identify, both because of his power and because of the distance. That he is evil is a given. That he does have power is a given.

"You have a lot of power. It is latent. It is in your inheritance and needs to be brought out. I am not a teacher, but I can perhaps help you realize your power. You are a good person. You will not misuse it, as so many do. You have the strength to resist this evil being brought. He knows he must stop you now, before you have the ability to overcome him.

"Some will be automatic. It is your inheritance. In times of great danger, there will be protections. You must know how to use and direct them or they will prove not enough."

"When a ball of fire was sent at me on the ship, I sent back a ball of water that stopped it. Nothing like that had even happened. I don't know how I did that."

"Your talent has intelligence attached to it. Your mind knows that water quenches fire. The fire was a perception, but so was the water. It was a visualization of two opposing forces. There was no fire and there was no water. There was something much more powerful.

"You said you see a flash across some people you meet. A snake or a dollar sign. That is the same. Your power is protecting you. You saw a skull and crossbones, such as the symbol on containers of poisons. It protected you. Your power cannot protect well from a poison in your drink or a knife in your heart.

"We will try to intensify your abilities where reading what people are is concerned. You must learn to see a chameleon or a mirage."

"Yes. A black nothing is a good way to hide in the night, but is rather obvious in daytime."

"You do not express such things well, do you?"

They both laughed.

"There is a psychological point about midnight on the full or dark moon. A pity there is neither tonight. We will begin examination for lessons in the morning. This evening, we will walk among the good people in the village and you will meet those who will become friends. Perhaps you will identify some who will not be friends, though I believe very few, if any such, to be here."

They did walk around the town. Will got the flash on only one person. Maybe it was a planted idea. A man who seemed affable and open had a chameleon flash across his face.

When they were back at the cottage, Will mentioned that he saw the flash.

"Tom Lecoufle. I know. He is what is referred to as two-faced. I have more faith in your ability, now. He is the only one we saw tonight who would cause such a thing. He did.

"We will begin in the morning."

They turned in for a restful night.

In the morning he walked along the beach with Bernadette at dawnlight. She liked to do that. It was very peaceful. They talked about various things, about what caused his flashes and so forth. The times something happened that brought out what might be a psychic experience. There were quite a lot. He had never considered them in quite the same way and hadn't realized how many times his talent had expressed itself.

"It is part of you. It is a reaction, usually. You do not realize when your body fights off a germ. It is a natural process. This kind of protection is no more nor less than the same thing."

They came to a pile of rocks with a couple of palm trees and some bananas growing on top. They sat on a flat rock to talk. There were a lot of various birds flitting around. A bright yellow small bird came to sit on the rocks just to one side. Will saw an ear and an old-style magnifying glass and Meerschaum pipe flash across it. Bernadette saw the look on his face and started to say something, but he shook his head very slightly and continued speaking. He had been talking about the way he felt at times when he was in a crowd and he somehow knew a thief or pickpocket was close. Sometimes he knew which person, sometimes not. He continued on, " ... the brighter shells. The sun ray clam and coquinas in Florida were like that."

Bernadette didn't need a stronger clue. She answered, "Some of the conchs here are beautiful. A cowry in the deeper water is very pretty, but can give a deadly sting.

"Well! There they are! The dolphins come to play right out there every morning. They are very happy animals."

They talked about dolphins a moment. Bernadette smiled and said, "Well, Arthur. It's time we got back to the house. A good slice of melon and some orange and pineapple chicha will be perfect!"

They stood and moved back along the beach. When

they were out of range, Bernadette asked what he saw. He told her.

"Hmm. The ear was obvious, but I don't know why the magnifying lens. Or the pipe."

"Sherlock Holmes. A magnifying glass and a Meerschaum pipe. I don't connect that with a little bird."

"Ah! And the ear. It was a detective, in your mind. It was seeking. I felt, seeing you saw an ear, that it was used to listen. That's why I called you Arthur. Your opponent knows you are near, but not where. The bird will probably go near everyone to listen until it locates you. I will call you Arthur, or Art, when we speak, if a name is necessary."

"I think maybe he'll only check on the people who contact or are with you. He's afraid I'll learn too much, and you're the one who could teach me."

She nodded. "It is fortunate that what you must know is mental. We won't have to demonstrate anything he could watch."

Will laughed. "So! You will be seen teaching me how to make medicines or such!"

"Yes. That will, as you say, throw him off the trail. We can use that to see if you can move things or only use perceptive reaction."

"I can move a very small feather or a piece of tissue paper barely big enough to see. Mom could do that. She said it wouldn't get stronger."

"Then we will have to develop your ability to detect poisons and such. It may not be needed, but it is better to prepare for a not-needed thing than to suddenly need it and not have it."

They spent the rest of the day with him learning to detect different things. Bernadette noted that it was linked to his sense of smell as well as to an undefined talent. By the end of the day he could detect hundreds of things. His ability to use his intensified senses could be directed. He was learning how. Bernadette used her abilities to influence thoughts to bring his talent out strongly.

They walked along the beach at dusk, then went to the village to chat and mingle.

In the morning Bernadette sat a bowl of cereal in front of him. He said, "Puffer fish toxin?"

She smiled. "You can sense it well. I would not have allowed you to taste it.

"Can you identify where it is in the bowl?"

"It's all through the bowl."

"You know it's there. Now I want you to use your ability to move small things. It is molecular in size. Move it a molecule at the time to this bowl." She sat a bowl of milk to the side.

He concentrated. After about five minutes he said he could visualize the molecule as a dot, but wasn't sure he could select the right ones to move.

"You know it's there. You know it's not a natural part of the bowl of cereal. Make your mind locate the proper molecule."

He concentrated again. He suddenly brightened. "I can do it! I can find whatever molecule I want! I make my sense of smell find it – and that's impossible!"

"It's impossible, yet you can do it. That is what your power is all about. It's why they call it magic.

He started moving the molecules. It would take forever to make any difference this way!

He could move about a tenth of a gram at once. He explained to Bernadette that he was ... " ... going to try to make the stuff that cures the parasite. That's about as hard to figure as anything you've taught me. It's toxic as Hell in minute quantities. I think diluting and using a drop of, say, thousand to one will do the trick, don't you?" He pointed to the bright yellow bird sitting on the windowsill with his thumb."

"That is the safest way. I'm glad you realize the method will let it deteriorate, but is useful if given within two hours."

They talked about medical plants until the bird flew away. Will concentrated and moved the selected molecules in groups. There was little of the poison in the bowl. It took him twelve minutes before he announced that there wasn't a molecule of the toxin left in the cereal. He ate the cereal. Bernadette said it was too bad he couldn't move that bowl of milk to the table of the person seeking him.

Next, they concentrated on him being able to confuse a mind, a talent Bernadette had, but he couldn't. Next was remote seeking, such as using the bird, but he had no talent for that. He had to be in the presence of the person.

They spent four more days looking for ways to use

his talent. He did have automatic protection in perception, such as with the fire and water incident.

"Your ability to move things can save you, but it will take time. You've been able to reduce the time to what can be a critical stage. You can now combine that with your identification ability.

"This is probably for nothing. When you need your talents, we have made them much stronger than they were. You are able to direct them and focus them, which makes you a very strong force. We have not awakened all your powers. We don't know what they are, but we have instituted a process where your mind can concentrate on a factor and you can overcome great obstacles. We have the focus to where your mind will solve problems much more rapidly.

"It is as much as I can do. I hope it is enough. I will aide you in some ways because of my abilities at remote manipulation. I can influence a mind that is attacking you if you identify that mind for me. We have a connection now, but it is a thing I can't define well. It is a connection between our talents.

"Mama Naomi has been in contact. A strange bird has been all over the ship recently. She and I believe a clue to your adversary is that he uses birds. His talent is in that. Be aware of that.

"We have arranged that you return to the ship. It is now leaving Curacao for Martinique, where you will go back aboard. Remember the bird and use what you have. I think your adversary will not know your talent is released a little and is developing. That will be natural.

"One thing about the type of person who schemes in these ways is that they have a power, but must be secure and certain of it. Cause a doubt and it weakens them."

"Mama Bernadette, I like you! You are a good person. Why do you have the reputation of the most powerful voodoo queen in the Caribbean?"

"It is feared by those of the ilk of your opponent. Good people do not fear my power. It is enough that they know I have it. It gives them pause.

"I will aid you in any way I can. Take the greatest care. This is not a children's game. You oppose true evil, as old-fashioned and trite as saying it may seem."

"If you ever need my help, if my little power can help you, it is here for your use."

She smiled. They hugged and Will headed for the little island hopper plane that would take him to Martinique.

Buck greeted him when he came up the ramp to the ship. Mama Naomi was on the center deck when they passed through. She chatted a moment. She had been in contact with a friend in New Orleans. There were only slight hints as to who Wila and Francine were plotting against.

A green parakeet flew to sit on a curtain rod above them. Buck said, "Well, Henry, the food here is as good as you'll find anywhere, and it's always there. You're going to gain ten pounds in a week."

The parakeet flew away.

"Bernadette warned us. We'll call you Henry," Naomi suggested. "We'll make a stop at St. Kitts, then out of Cancun, then New Orleans. Bernadette wants me to work with you a little. She wants you to read everyone, trying to expand the distance they have to be from you before you can't read them."

He agreed, then went to his cabin. Buck was with him as they unlocked the door. The parakeet was sitting on a vase of dried flowers six feet away. Buck got an evil grin on his face. He said, "The guy who had the cabin first, Will Farmer, caught a plane back to the states. Houston, I believe. He was a little strange. He could know all about a person with a glance. It was scary, at first, but he was a great guy when you got to know him.

"See you in the entertainment room in an hour? Do you play pool?"

"A little. Bar tables. Bets? No way!"

"Drinks, and they're free, anyhow."

"You're on!"

He went inside and relaxed a bit.

After a few games of eight ball, he and Buck went to the upper deck to the pool and showed off a bit. They were both hits with the women. Will could take one look and see what they were up to. Most were looking for a good time, a few had the dollar signs, one had a spider flash across her face.

Will decided she was trying to get a man in her web. She was about forty, attractive, but losing it. He told Buck. She was wealthy and a schemer. Maybe Buck could get a few dollars and give her a good time, whether that was what she was after or not.

A little later he met a girl from California who was rather stunning – and knew it. She was playing to it the way he was playing to his good physique and charm. She had an otter flash across her face.

Otter?

Oh, yeah. Otters were one of the few animals that made life a fun game. They played all the time. This could be a great night!

It was.

In the morning they were at St. Kitts. They stayed four hours, then headed into the Caribbean.

The parakeet that had been on the boat since Will

first left it for Isla Palmitas was suddenly not there anymore. Will wondered if it was now in Houston.

How would it find him in a city that size?

Two things: the closeness to whoever made it easier, or it would be a waiting game for him.

He got an urge to call Mama Bernadette. It came from nowhere. He made the call.

"Will, your adversary's name is Liam LeFevre. He is in New Orleans. His place is just outside, on the way to the lake. He has all the Cajuns terrified of him. With reason. He has no normal emotions.

"He may be able to fool your sense of identity. He is powerful, but he doesn't have the talents he wants people to think he has. There probably isn't anyone in that area who knows half as much about poisons as he does. He is also a fencing expert and knows hand-to-hand martial arts.

"It is possible he thinks he is safe from you. He thinks you are in another state and would have come to New Orleans if you didn't fear a confrontation."

"Thanks, Bernadette. I'll use that to shake him a bit. Is there a way to make him believe ... that I know where anything directed at me originates?"

"What do you mean?"

"The watcher birds. I know where such things come from. My identification talent tells me. I have powers no one knows about. I might be the one playing the cat, not him."

"Playing the ... oh. Cat and mouse?"

"Uh-huh. He's caught and I'm playing the cruelty

game cats play with their prey sometimes."

She giggled. "Scare the holy living piss out of him – and make him doubt his power at the same time. Very good!

"Remember the poisons."

"That, you can rest assured of."

They chatted a minute more. Will made another call. To Copa Airlines. Cancun. A quick flight to Houston from there, then a connecting flight to New Orleans.

He talked with Buck and Naomi. They had a good time until Cancun, then Will was gone. They wished him the best and would help in any way they could.

It was drizzling when he got off the plane in New Orleans. He hadn't been able to get a picture or very good description of LeFevre. He didn't doubt LeFevre had a way to know he was coming in on that plane.

He didn't look like him. He looked much older and had a paunch. He had a Van Dyke beard and wore flashy jewelry. He had a tendency to talk out of the side of his mouth, which tended to look like he was sneering at you. His motions were exaggerated and he looked at all the young boys a little too intensely.

Will knew a lot of disguises from the carnival days.

A suave type of man, maybe thirty years old, very much in shape, came to him at the baggage rack. Will got no flash, so this was LeFevre.

"Mr. Farmer?"

"Eh? Oh, yeah. What?"

"I was supposed to meet a Wilson Farmer on this

flight. We call him Will. It was to be a surprise, but you aren't the same Wilson Farmer. I guess the joke's on me!"

"Maybe because I'm Wilber Farmer. You can see why I use Will. Wilber is a Hell of a name to be stuck with."

"Well, shit! That fucks up my surprise. Thank you very much!"

"What? My fault? You nuts or just stupid?"

"Nobody calls me stupid!" he hissed.

"I just did. You're a fucking loon on top of it! Get out of my face!" He grabbed his suitcase and walked off. LeFevre made some signs at his back. He saw the ball of fire coming at him. He turned, held up a hand, made like he was rolling something into a ball, and flicked it toward LeFevre with a goathead sign, meanwhile sending the perception water ball at it.

"Raised in Haiti. Know a thing or two. Back at you, Asshole!"

He walked on out. LeFevre was staring at him in almost shock, real fear showing on his face.

That would raise a doubt or two in his mind! Some fat pedophile with an attitude thwarted his big bad curse?

Will went out and into the restaurant, then to the restroom. He went into a stall and came out ten minutes later as himself.

He was reading everyone around him, now. The pretty waitress had a candle flash. That was romantic. That woman was a snake, that man an unformed blob.

That probably meant he was blah.

E=mc2 flashed across that face. Scientist or genius.

A blob of slime. Several thieves of one sort or another. The spider.

It was surprising how many had a cash register flash. Greedy for money.

He had a burger and fries, then went to his apartment. He would rest a bit, then go to a couple of places up toward the lake. He was going to make this look like, really, what it was! He was the one doing the challenging!

LeFevre would know his talents wouldn't be much help, and he was in doubt about them, now. Will came back the way he did to force the issue and make LeFevre react much sooner than he wanted to.

This was still not a game. He must convince himself of his abilities and remain strong in his confidence.

No problem! Mama Bernadette had made that damned certain.

A little bird came to sit on his windowsill.

"Greetings! Yes, I'm back. Maybe we can face each other and get you over with, hmmm?"

The bird flew off. He grinned.

Now to review things in his mind. The hard part was still in the future. He wanted it to be soon, to get it over with.

Tonight might be interesting. LeFevre was going to have to try something outside his talent area.

Or was he?

Will would see how he acted. He would know better

than to trust that one a millimeter. He could end up dead.

He laid back and put his mind in a suspended state. He could do that for years. He simply stopped consciously thinking. He was floating. Nothing else.

At five thirty he got up, showered, shaved, dressed for a casual night and went to Helene's Haven for a beer, then toward the lake. A little sparrow was by the curb when he got in the cab. He looked at it and said, "Hi! I'm heading for Paulo's Palace for a gourmet meal." He got in the cab and said, "Paulo's Palace."

"I heard you the first time. I ain't deaf."

"But I wasn't talking to you. I was talking to that buzzard sitting on the fence. It's a demon who keeps driving me crazy! I can't find who sent it, but whoever it is better hope I never do! Maybe I know somebody who can send them a demon or two, myself! Maybe a Glock forty demon."

"But there wasn't no ... okay." The driver was in for a very nervous fifteen minutes. Will was already in the cab. He was obviously crazy as a loon. A Glock forty might mean he was carrying. A nut with a gun. Just what I need!

He was finally there. The cabbie didn't try the "Fifty dollars for outside the city" bit. That might be stupid beyond belief. He said, "Twenty two fifty." Will gave him a twenty and a five and waved, then went into the restaurant.

LeFevre was sitting at a table on the terrace. He went directly over to say, "Will Farmer. I was on the flight before. A guy didn't show up in time.

"I suppose you were at that one. You did send the bird to my apartment.

"Oh. I knew it was you from on the ship. I can sense where a watcher like that came from."

"There was a Will Farmer on that flight. Did you know that? Wilber, not Wilson. A fat pig with some power from when he was in Haiti."

"My life is full of that kind of thing. I guess that's why I had the sudden urge to come home. I sensed that there would be some kind of thing. Having a talent or two can be confusing, but it can be fun. I keep finding more and more things that tell me more and more other things.

"You don't wonder how I came in and knew this was you?"

"I assumed you'd seen me somewhere, or that your talent said it was me."

"In a way. You're the only one here who's blocked."

"Well, shall we order and discuss things?"

"Don't see why not. We can be civilized about it. Maybe you can tell me why you decided to concentrate on me. What do I know that I don't know I know about you?"

"I'll see if it's safe to tell you after we talk a bit.

"The paella here is famous. I'll have that. Rose wine. Chateau Brianfeld fifty five."

"I'll have lobster chowder. I've had enough paella lately. The wine will be very good for both dishes."

They ordered. They chatted about the cruise and

Haiti and Jamaica. LeFevre said he heard there was a voodoo woman on Isla Palmitas who terrorized the whole Caribbean.

"Mama Bernadette? She doesn't terrorize anyone. The ones who're so afraid of her are the ones who deserve to be terrorized. Slime. She's really a very nice, educated woman with a lot of power. She doesn't use it much, but everyone knows she can and will."

Their orders came. The waitress was shaky and scared. Will saw a screaming face in a flash. When she put his bowl in front of him, he saw the poison sign.

There was something in the chowder. She was terrorized into putting it in. She wanted to warn him, but didn't know how. He tried to send her something to assure her it was under control.

The wine came. He sat back to sip it slowly. So did LeFevre.

He said the chowder had to cool. It didn't have the flavor if you ate it too soon.

LeFevre said the opposite was true of paella. Did Will object if he ate now?

"Of course not."

Will found the poison. It was extremely heavy. It would take a few minutes to move it. There wasn't much, so it was something very potent.

He sipped the wine, tested the chowder, said it wasn't quite ready yet, then sipped the rest of the wine. LeFevre poured him another glass. He tested the chowder again, said it was ready, and ate it as LeFevre finished his paella.

LeFevre ordered flan for both of them, then sat back to wait for Will to finish the chowder. They ate the flan, then ordered coffee and cognac with a touch of mint.

"Well, now to business," LeFevre said, smirking. "I don't think we need part as enemies. You are here because of Wila and Francine, but I can assure you they were using you as pawn all along. Francine was using you as a pawn in another way. She had a boyfriend on the side that she was using to increase her power. She was pregnant with his child, as you know.

"He was using her, in turn. She thought she was getting power from him, and did. A little.

"He was getting power from her. A lot. She was more powerful than any of you knew.

"Except you?"

Will shrugged.

"Well, let me tell you a story, then I have to go.

"I was raised by a woman who was much feared for her talent. She used a lot of trickery, but did have some small ability at fortune telling. She used various chemicals to make people think she could put curses on this one and take a curse off that one and so forth. She crossed the wrong person with that and ended up strangled.

"She taught me a lot of what I know. I always had a lot more talent than she did, and she was truly a disgusting example of a human being.

"I'm no prize. There's what some would consider a lack in me. I don't feel much. That's been both good and bad for me. I won't fall in love and get everything I have taken away by one of what too many women are. I guess that's the way it's always been and always will be. Nature. Secure your future.

"I didn't feel anything when my mother was killed. Maybe a little relief. She was never good to me. She blamed me for her not having power. She blamed me for her not having money. She blamed me when she had a headache.

"I turned myself off, emotionally. I felt a little rush when she was killed. I know she poisoned a few people. It seemed to give her a rush. There's that in me. I admit I've killed before, and that it was a rush. Wila and Francine were a much better rush.

"I learned how to convince people I had magical power to kill or to cause unbearable pain or even to send them directly to Hell. Most of the theatricality is to convince people a trickery is real.

"Francine was my sister. My father impregnated my mother and Wila at about the same time. He was using the voodoo sex rituals to control a number of women.

"My father is the only one I haven't triumphed over in life. I have two pictures of him, but they show him to be about my age now, though my mother said he was known for more than fifty years before he met her.

"There is no longer anything in the way to my getting his immortality. I've studied everything from Apollonius of Tyana to Gilgamesh and onward. There is a ritual that can pass his immortality to a son. He dies and it is in me.

"You could thwart me in this. Francine could detect your latent talents and told me a number of times that you could defeat me. Few others could. None of the others would, but you have a sense of morality that they lack.

"Wila was using Francine to keep control of you. She said they could release your power if anything happened to either. I knew that was possibly true, but you were going outside their range of influence. That you have that power is obvious in that you stopped my attempt to kill you as you left their area of influence. I knew I was going to kill both of them and wanted you out of the way.

"That power is, apparently, not so strong as I had believed. That other Will Farmer was able to turn it away, and he had no powers I could detect. He said he learned how in Haiti, so it was probably from a woman known as Mama Bernadette. She has more power than almost anyone. I'll stay clear of her influence until I have my immortality, then will also have power to protect myself. I won't father any sons, so my immortality will go on."

"Why?" Will asked.

"Why?"

"Why would you want immortality? I would think life would be intolerably boring after a hundred years or so. You contribute nothing to the world. You are negative. Why would you want to go on and on like that?"

"I suppose you wouldn't grab immortality if you could! Yeah, right!"

"I wouldn't want it. I could have it. I could possibly seek a long life if I was serving a purpose, but not just go on and on without any.

"So! Does the reason you think I'm no problem have to do with the stuff you forced the waitress to put in the chowder?"

"Thallium. The amount you consumed is irreversible."

"But I didn't consume any. You did. I moved it to your paella while I waited for the chowder to cool.

"Want to tell me about your father a bit more? Surely you know that you and Francine wouldn't be the only ones he fathered. Surely you know that others would have the same kind of plots. He was around at least fifty years before you were born. You were born with some talent. We can assume it was from both him and your mother, seeing you've stated that you had more power than she did."

LeFevre stared at him. "No. You couldn't move it."

"Okay. Then you won't die from it. Your father? If he only did it to you and no others were harmed, I'd let it go. He didn't. You drew others into it. You said you'd killed others. Wila bragged that she did. Your mother did. Francine probably did.

"How many others?"

LeFevre was staring. "You can't make me manufacture symptoms with psychology!"

"Okay. Your father?"

"He's in this area, but spends time on the islands and in Central America. You never know where he is. He's got a following under a lot of different names in different places. That way, he doesn't get the attention of people like Mama Bernadette.

"He's perfected control and methods. He's got a cruel streak. He tortures, which I won't do. If it's necessary for a person to die, kill them. Don't torture, though there were two where I was sorely tempted. He killed some people with a circus because they had powers they were hiding, if what my mother said was true. She said they were posing as fortune tellers, but really did have a vision about your future. The woman had spotted him because he had no set future. He feared they would combine their power to oppose him. He killed six others when he caused a bus driver to swerve in front of a gasoline tanker. It exploded and killed everyone. Eight killed because he was afraid of two.

"I suspect he's fathered a lot of children. I know of one other in Guatemala and one in Haita. Those because my mother tried to trace him and found out about them.

"I don't know much more. I know what he looks like. He's suave and handsome and very charming. He's a monster in sheep's clothing. He has more power than anyone else in the world, I think.

"I think he's very good with disguises. I don't think he's actually a changeling, but he can ... project an image.

"Did you really move the thallium?"

"Yes."

"Funny. I was afraid of you because of the power. I don't feel much about the fact that, if you did, I'll die within three days. It's more interesting than scary. I'm a little sad that I won't be immortal. I think I want to go on to try to find something ... to find a purpose, as you suggested."

Will saw the flash of a pistol across his face. He tensed.

"I think maybe I want some revenge, but even that's not strong. Maybe I'll get a little rush from killing you."

He pulled a pistol from under the table to point square between Will's eyes.

"Maybe. I don't think you've thought things through

very well," Will said. "What you've failed to see is that ... yes?"

He was looking over LeFevre's shoulder. LeFevre started to turn, then back to Will. The pistol was pointed very slightly to the side. Will lifted the table sharply, spilling the dishes and glasses into LeFevre's lap as he moved sharply to the side. The pistol fired, nicking him a bit on the shoulder. LeFevre was going over backward and fired again, but this one was at the ceiling. Will pushed the table on top of him and swung a chair into his face. He was knocked unconscious by the chair.

People were screaming and babbling. Will yelled, "My God! He's crazy! I didn't go after *her*, she came after *me*! She said she wasn't going with anyone! My God! He tried to *shoot* me! My God!"

The waitress ran to say he had better get to a doctor, fast. He put something into the food. Her eyes were pleading.

"I know. I expected that, I know what poison it was, so it was easy to take the antidote before, but, my God!"

The gate guard rushed in, brandishing his own pistol. He heard shots! What was going on?

"You're hurt!" the waitress cried. There was a small bit of blood from his shoulder.

"It barely broke the skin. I hate to think if had been two inches to the left!"

The gate guard put handcuffs on LeFevre. He said no one was to touch anything. Don't touch the gun.

Fingerprints.

"Oh, Sam, get real! Everyone in the place saw what happened!" the waitress said.

A woman had a cell phone. She had called the police. Five minutes.

The police came in eight minutes, took statements from everyone, and took LeFevre to the cage in the squad car. Will was right beside the door while the cops finished their on-the-spot reports. LeFevre said, "So. What's the story?"

"You thought I stole your girlfriend and went nuts."

"Okay. You won all around. You'll go after my father. He's using the name Perez in Guatemala and Martin in Jamaica. He's supposed to be in Honduras, then will come back here. He's Wentworth here, this time.

"This will be a new experience for me. One last thing before I die.

"What will they think when I die of thallium poisoning, do you suppose?"

"Maybe they'll think it's what caused you to go apeshit in there."

He grinned. "Could be!"

A cop saw him there, talking. He ran over and said they weren't supposed to talk.

"It's okay. He's been feeling depressed and confused. He doesn't know why he did that. Arlene went with anything in pants. He doesn't know why I bothered him, but he's having a lot of things go wrong the last few days.

"I don't suppose it would be possible for me to not bring any charges?"

"Well, for the shooting at you, but the restaurant's the one who's bringing charges. They sort of frown on people who shoot the place up."

LeFevre grinned. "Happens a lot?"

"Nope. First time." He grinned, too. LeFevre did have charm.

Will went home about an hour later. This was a night he didn't ever want to happen again.

Will called Bernadette to report. He called the ship and talked with Buck and Naomi.

Bernadette said she couldn't find where he was or what name he was using. If he were to come as close as Haiti, she might be able to find him with the talent.

Will suggested she use her contacts. Don't do anything, but let him know where to find him. He would have a reputation with the women and would tend to cruelties and fear, but he would be playing his powers down. LeFevre had shown him one of the pictures. The man was sort of ruggedly handsome, had a good build, but was rather average in features. He looked about thirty years old.

He told her there was a personal reason he was looking for this one. LeFevre had let something slip. It had to do with his parents' deaths. But for that, he would have let it end with LeFevre.

Naomi said there were stories of a man who never aged in the islands. He would come maybe once in two years. He always looked the same. She had seen him once, when she was about ten years old. He did look a lot like the picture he'd sent on the net, so far as she could remember.

Will suggested that some fortune teller had spotted him because he had no set future. That could help.

She spotted *him* because he didn't have a set future!

Bernadette promised to try to locate him through the stories. It was a good thing to use on the older people who might have seen him more than once. She had contacts in Central America and Southern Mexico, particularly Yucatan and Oaxaca. She might be able to find a pattern if people noted when he was in a place and where he went next.

If he discovered he was being looked for, he would protect – or he would challenge. He was supposed to be very strong. He had managed to live a very long time.

There wasn't much to do but wait. Will would try to develop his talents. He could strengthen himself in some areas because of the confrontation with LeFevre. He would, for once in his life, set out to kill someone directly, not just let them, as in LeFevre's case, kill themselves.

His parents were killed when the bus they were in was hit by a gasoline tanker. It exploded and killed them and six others.

Bernadette called to say she might have a lead. Cuba. A man was in Southern Cuba who fit the description, as did five hundred others there. This one came every couple of years. He had been coming, so far as the informant knew, for thirty five or more years. They called him Viejo Joven. He never changed.

"Viejo Joven means young old man," she explained. "He was in Cuba nine months ago. A witch woman had a baby, supposed to be his, a week ago. She's bitter because she claims he stole most of her power

"That could be, Will. It's possible he doesn't have as much power as his reputation. That would be why he plays them down. He finds a woman with power and uses the method to steal it. It doesn't increase his power anymore. It lessens theirs. It also results in LeFevres. A mother who resents the child and hates the father at its expense.

"It also means he hasn't powers as strong as mine. He would have been after me a long time ago if he did.

"It's also possible he tried. I've had my share of propositions. He would be experienced enough at hiding his power that I wouldn't know unless I had reason to read him. Most of them seemed normal horny men. Some of them were very charming. I didn't look further."

"Would anyone have a hint as to where he went from there?"

"Mama Ana has some photos. She'll e-mail them to me. I'll forward them. We'll know more what he looks like. She says there are other women he slept with. It's possible she can find something. I've spoken with her some. I hope to be able to stop the child having to pay for what his mother and father are."

They chatted for awhile. Then it was back to waiting. Will contacted everyone he knew who might have a connection with voodoo or psychic powers. Most of them knew there was a non-aging papaloi. Anyone of them who spoke Spanish had heard of

Viejo Joven. Most thought it was just an extension of the Gilgamesh legend. A myth.

Buck called. He said the pictures Bernadette sent were a shock. That man had been on several tours. The crew knew of him. They said he was a little demanding, but not bad. One crewmember, just before retirement age, said he recalled twice when people died on the ship for no reason they could find. He was aboard both times.

"Is Naomi there?" Will asked.

"She's in the other room. Just a sec." She came on a minute later. Will asked if that man had approached her.

"I think maybe yah, Mon. He done looked differnt from what he looked. From the power. I think he false, but him another man what want a piece of ass, so I smile 'n say I don't want no cruise romance. I no let him know I got me power. I does know ways to hide it."

"Did he get off on any of the tours on some special ... I guess you wouldn't know."

Buck came on and said there was a call for Naomi on the computer. He would see what he could dig up and would call if he got anything Will could use. He and Bernadette were in contact at least once per day, so they might be able to come up with something.

"Wait! Here's Ma. She's excited."

Naomi came on. "I got me a friend on other boat, Mon. He tell me this one use name Jose Martin. He for New Orleans for one week. He be where you be."

"Maybe I can find him in town. He would contact ... no one. He hasn't left a trail of laughter here in the past."

"Yoni, he say Martin tell girl he got house on south of lake. Swamp there, but he got island. Yoni hear when he bring drink to Martin and girl. Girl look Cajun."

"An island in the big swamp. That seems to fit him to perfection.

"Did he leave any message for me?"

"Message? What? You done gone loco?"

"He wouldn't be overheard unless he meant to be overheard. He doesn't come here much, even though he apparently owns a place close. He's challenging me. He wants to face me on home ground, so to speak. Maybe I'll accommodate him!"

"You be careful! He ain't no amateur! He got lots of experience, Mon! Slow it down!

"Buck, he on other phone. He say call Mama Bernadette. Now!"

He rang off and immediately called Mama Bernadette. She said she knew she couldn't talk him out of facing Martin. It would be dangerous, but there were a few things that could help.

"Wear iron, as soft as you can find, and silver. You don't need much, but it can disrupt some powers to a slight extent.

"Will, he knows you have power. He doesn't know which. He will do something to make you tell him things. He uses poisons and hypnotism.

"You can block him the same way he can block you. He won't know what you can do unless you demonstrate it for him. You know some of his powers.

"Go slow. He will try to make you go fast. It is easier to defend while the opponent is off balance – so don't get off balance. Do *not* allow him to anger you to an uncontrollable point. That is defeat.

"Have you practiced with your automatic defenses? Have you been able to strengthen them?"

"Yes. I've learned to call specific ones out. I've learned how to block entirely. It's there. I picture myself inside a steel sphere."

"He can sense, but I don't think he can read with any accuracy.

"Will, you are a good person. You are going to as much as face Satan in person. Don't let it change what you are if you survive this. I have to say your chances are less than fifty-fifty, but you are resourceful. I will aid in any way I can. Naomi will, and several others. Many of us with a talent past the small things can sense a terrible danger, but we also have hope in the feelings.

"Take the greatest care."

"That, I can promise. I didn't want to ever be in any position remotely like this, but I am. I'm what I am. I have to face it. Win or lose, he's going to know he was in a fight!"

She gave a few more warnings, then Will called Buck and Naomi to say it may be goodbye or it may be a turn to a brighter time. That was corny, but it was what he felt.

He got some soft iron filings and rubbed them into his clothes. They would itch, but were necessary. He put some old silver quarters and dimes in his pockets.

Then he called a taxi, thought better of it, and rented a budget car.

Then he headed for the Big Swamp.

There would be something to lead him directly to the place. He didn't doubt that for one second.

He also suspected Martin was a very good actor, that he had some powers, but depended on chemicals and hypnotism, as Bernadette had suggested.

He was just at the city limits when he thought of something. He considered it.

No. He wouldn't know. LeFevre was in a coma. He would die before dawn tomorrow. His mind was gone. If Martin had the power to read, there wouldn't be anything there.

This was to be a confrontation to the death. He or Martin would walk – or crawl – away. Not both.

An hour later he was on the Big Swamp road. There are only a few side roads. It is dangerous to stop.

As he drove slowly past the third side road a bright flash showed.

It wasn't his talent. It was a flash from a flashbulb or something. He was supposed to think it was psychic, but he had trained himself to know when it was his talent.

He drove into the swamp to see a large house on a little island. There were a number of places he could pull off to one side or the other and remain unseen from the house.

That he was seen was obvious. That flash.

A car went by behind him on the main road. There was a flash.

Martin had a radar setup that made the flash anytime a car went by. That was a power he didn't have or was weak in him. That would mean he didn't necessarily know Will was there.

Or was a trick to make him think that. In either case, he would be expected to go very slowly and stealthily toward the house, probably on foot from a direction away from that entrance road.

Will grinned. He drove on to the front of the house to park beside an old Jeep. He honked the horn and got out.

Martin came to the door to stare at him for a few seconds. He wasn't well-protected. Will saw swirls and spirals. Martin was confused.

"Hello. I'm Will Farmer. You killed my parents a bit over four years ago."

Fear? Ah! Project absolute confidence. He's off balance. He's confused that subterfuge isn't part of this equation!

He recovered. "Come on in. We can discuss things in the past."

Will grinned and almost sauntered to the door and inside.

"Can I offer refreshments? I have soda, lemonade, wine, beer – what have you."

"Lemonade sounds good. It's a little warm today. The humidity in these swamps can make it unpleasant."

The house was air conditioned. It was cool, but was hot and humid outside. Martin poured a glass of lemonade for Will and one for himself. He asked if Will would like a bit of vodka in it. He poured a little from a bottle of Smirnoff into his own. Will nodded. He poured in a bit and handed Will the glass. Will smiled and said, "But without scopolamine, please?"

Martin laughed and poured the lemonade down the sink and poured another. He added vodka from another bottle. This was only lemonade and vodka.

Martin started talking about his recent trip to Cuba in a droning voice. He was waving his glass slowly back and forth. Will acted like he was succumbing to the hypnotism for a few minutes. He could see Martin's confidence returning.

Let him think it was working? Shake him by grinning and taking a drink of the lemonade?

Give it another few minutes.

Martin stopped talking, looked at Will sitting there, drooping.

"I am playing cowboys and Indians with you. I will tie you up. It is part of the game."

He brought some Twist-Ties from a drawer and secured Will's hands and feet to the chair.

"You will now answer my questions truthfully and completely.

"What are your powers?"

"I can read minds. I can cause your heart to stop beating. I can sense what is in a drink or food. I know your real nature. You are a pig and greedy and have no purpose in life. You are empty and have no real feelings about anything. You don't know why you want to live forever. You are bored and tired. I can make your body heat up until it burns. I can...."

"Stop!"

"Resist hypnotism."

"So. I don't know how much of what you said is true."

"Most of it. I just couldn't resist reading what your life is. I'd rather be dead."

"That will be soon. You can't get out of that chair."

Will had been removing very small pieces of the Twist-Ties since they were put on. The little flanges that made them work. All he had to do was make the sharp director ends a tiny bit smoother. The flanges wouldn't hold. He lifted his hands and moved his feet away from the chair.

"Oh?"

That shook Martin!

"You had a lot of people fooled about your power. The only one you really have is to keep yourself alive and young. Maybe a little of the regular powers, but not strong. You use trickery and chemicals and hypnotism."

He saw the pistol flash across Martin's face.

"You can try. Remember what happened to LeFevre, your son, or one of them, when he tried to shoot me.

"You disappoint me. I thought this might be a difficult confrontation, that there might be a little doubt about the outcome. You're a clever trickster with a directed talent of personal survival. You have no emotions."

He thought about what he had said about stopping a heart. The beat was an electrical impulse along a nerve. Could he actually stop it?

He concentrated. He didn't have the ability to detect which nerve. He could stop that minute an electrical current.

He experimented. He stopped different ones as he talked about the emptiness that was Jose Martin, regardless of which name he was using at a given moment.

Martin was reaching toward the pistol very slowly. He suddenly jerked and gasped.

"I told you I can stop your heart. I also warned you about pistols."

A black belt flashed across Martin's face. Will remembered he was a karate expert.

He couldn't stop Martin's heart for long enough to do more than cause the discomfort. "Sit back and relax. We can talk or end it now. Your call."

Martin sat back. He was wary. Will saw a fox flash across Martin's face. He was going to try a little trickery.

There was a cigarette pack on the little table. Will saw a concentration on that. Martin asked if he could smoke. Will nodded. There was a dart across Martin's face for a tenth of a second.

The cigarettes would have some kind of poisonous

dart inside. Martin didn't smoke. There were none of the tars or chemicals in that room a smoker would leave.

What poison? It would have to be fast and definite for him to try anything like this.

Curare. Very small amounts are effective.

Martin was fumbling with the cigarettes. He was selecting a certain one. Will concentrated while seeming to sit back to wait.

Martin selected the cigarette, then picked up the matches. It seemed there was water on the counter. The matches were wet. Will had made the water spill when Martin got the vodka. He didn't know, at that time, the matches would be used, but he wasn't taking any chances here.

Martin went to the bar and found a lighter in a drawer and came to sit back to light the cigarette.

This wasn't so clever. If he was looking for a light he would have taken the cigarette to the counter and used the lighter there. Martin was getting desperate. It gave Will time to finish moving the curare.

Martin picked up the cigarette and lit the lighter. The cigarette was pointing directly at Will. Martin blew sharply. a tiny dart was sticking in Will's arm.

He picked it out and handed it to Martin, who was pale and shaking. He looked like he really would have a heart attack. Will tried the stop that had brought the gasp. Martin clutched at his heart and fell to the side. He was laying on the floor, sobbing. He pleaded with Will to let him live.

"Because you have a pact with Satan, in your mind, and this will deliver you to him directly." He sent another stop. Martin gasped and sobbed.

Stop it! This is torture! This is not what I am!

"Tell Satan hello for me!" He sent the fireball at Martin, who screamed and jerked. He was dead.

Will went out to the car and drove back to New Orleans.

"So that was the end of it. I expected it would be a pretty hairy confrontation. If I'd believed he had the power, it would have been. If he *had* the power, it would have been!

"He thought he had made a pact with the devil. He didn't really want to live anymore, but was convinced to die was to go to Hell. Without recourse."

"You don't believe that's where he is?" Buck asked. They were all at Mama Bernadette's place for a little reunion and victory party.

"No. I think the idea's downright silly. He lived in Hell right here and was prolonging his stay there. I would let that continue if he didn't insist on bringing others into it. He was making lives programmed to live in Hell.

"He was an empty shell. I sat there and saw how pathetic he was. I caught myself using a little torture at the end, but he was living in torture. I actually stopped that for him. If there's a continuation, he's probably better off dead."

"There be Hell, Mon, but you got that right!" Naomi declared. "It be Hell we makes for ourself. He be better die to get *out* of Hell!"

"Well, the future looks better for all of us with him gone," Bernadette said. "He was, as you say, purely pathetic at the end."

"He be pure pathetic from start to end."

"I wish I knew his story. What were his parents like?" Buck asked.

"I agree," Will answered. "It will be a lot like LeFevre. He probably knocked off his father for the power or something as sick. Maybe this will end it. I don't want all that power he didn't have for me to steal.

"I also wonder if this hasn't been going on for centuries, if Gilgamesh wasn't the original Viejo Joven and this is the end of a direct line through most of history."

"Some of them were good. Maybe they got the power by doing what you did. Got rid of an evil, only they had the power to take the power of their father," Buck suggested. "Some were good, some were evil. I suspect the greed for immortality was a driving force that they every one regretted before it was over."

"Just so it's over," Will said. "I hereby tender any powers I have to Mama Bernadette, to use for the good of all.

"Am I obsequious or what?"

They all gave him the finger.

C. D. Moulton's works are available on most major outlets as printed or e-books. CD writes the CD Grimes, PI, mysteries, the Det. Lt. Nick Storie mysteries, the Clint Faraday mysteries, the Flight of the Maita science fiction series, books on orchid culture and many others of many types. Mystery, adventure, intrigue, science fiction, humor, fantasy, paranormal, mild erotica, and factual.